A Piece of Cake

To dear Pat Tupper and all the family,
with tons of love as ever

J. M.

Second U.S. paperback edition 1998

The Library of Congress has cataloged the first paperback edition as follows:

Murphy, Jill.
A piece of cake / Jill Murphy. — 1st U.S. paperback ed.
Summary: When Mama Elephant puts her family on a diet, their willpower
remains strong until Granny sends a cake.
ISBN 0-7636-0111-X
[1. Weight control–Fiction. 2. Elephants–Fiction.] I. Title.
[PZ7.M9534Pi 1997]
[E]–dc20   96-26251

2 4 6 8 10 9 7 5 3 1

Printed in Hong Kong

This book was typeset in M Bembo.
The pictures were done in colored pencil.

Candlewick Press
2067 Massachusetts Avenue
Cambridge, Massachusetts 02140

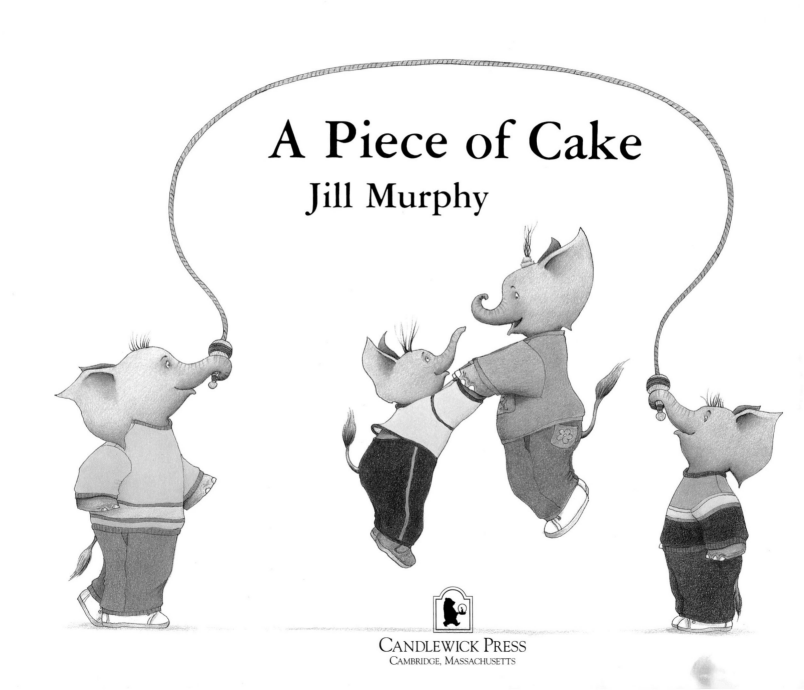

A Piece of Cake

Jill Murphy

CANDLEWICK PRESS
CAMBRIDGE, MASSACHUSETTS

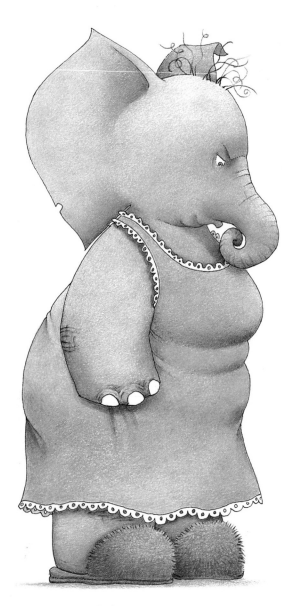

"I'm fat," said Mrs. Large.

"No you're not," said Lester.

"You're our cuddly mommy," said Laura.

"You're *just* right," said Luke.

"Mommy's got wobbly bits," said the baby.

"Exactly," said Mrs. Large. "As I was saying – I'm fat."

"We must all go on a diet," said Mrs. Large. "No more cake. No more cookies. No more potato chips. No more sitting around all day. From now on, it's healthy living."

"Can we watch TV?" asked Lester, as they trooped in from school.

"Certainly not!" said Mrs. Large. "We're all off for a nice healthy jog around the park."

And they were.

"What's our snack, Mom?" asked Laura
when they arrived home.
"Some nice healthy watercress soup," said
Mrs. Large. "Followed by a nice healthy cup
of water."
"Oh!" said Laura. "That sounds . . . nice."

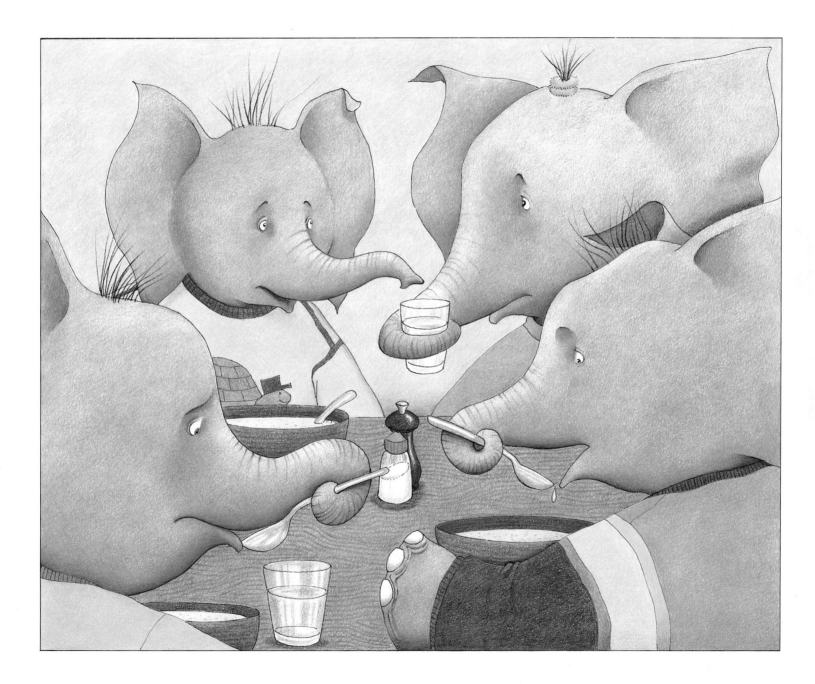

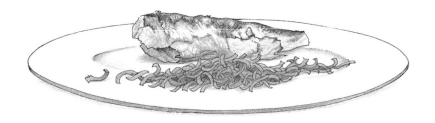

"I'm just going to watch the news, dear,"
said Mr. Large when he came home from work.
"No you're not, dear," said Mrs. Large.
"You're off for a nice healthy jog around
the park, followed by supper – delicious
fish with grated carrots."
"I can't wait," said Mr. Large.

It was awful. Every morning there was a healthy breakfast followed by exercises. Then there was a healthy snack followed by a healthy jog. By the time evening came everyone felt terrible.

"We aren't getting any thinner, dear,"
said Mr. Large.

"Perhaps elephants are *meant* to be fat,"
said Luke.

"Nonsense!" said Mrs. Large. "We mustn't
give up now."

"Wibbly wobbly wibbly wobbly," went
the baby.

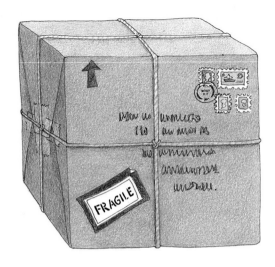

One morning a parcel arrived. It was a cake
from Granny. Everyone stared at it hopefully.
Mrs. Large put it into the cupboard on a high
shelf. "Just in case we have visitors," she
said sternly.

Everyone kept thinking about the cake.
They thought about it during the healthy jog.
They thought about it during supper.
They thought about it in bed that
night. Mrs. Large sat up. "I can't stand
it anymore," she said to herself. "I must
have a piece of that cake."

Mrs. Large crept out of bed and went
downstairs to the kitchen. She took a knife
out of the drawer and opened the cupboard.
There was only one piece of cake left!

"Ah ha!" said Mr. Large, seeing the knife.
"Caught in the act!"
Mrs. Large switched on the light and saw
Mr. Large and all the children hiding
under the table.
"There *is* one piece left," said Laura in
a helpful way.

Mrs. Large began to laugh. "We're all as
bad as each other!" she said, eating the
last piece of cake before anyone else did.
"I do think elephants are meant to be fat,"
said Luke.
"I think you're probably right, dear," said
Mrs. Large.
"Wibbly wobbly wibbly wobbly!" went
the baby.

MONSTER CAN'T SLEEP

Virginia Mueller

pictures by Lynn Munsinger

Puffin Books

PUFFIN BOOKS
Published by the Penguin Group
Viking Penguin Inc., 40 West 23rd Street, New York, New York 10010, U.S.A.
Penguin Books Ltd, 27 Wrights Lane, London W8 5TZ England
Penguin Books Australia Ltd, Ringwood, Victoria, Australia
Penguin Books Canada Ltd, 2801 John Street, Markham, Ontario, Canada L3R 1B4
Penguin Books (N.Z.) Ltd, 182–190 Wairau Road, Auckland 10, New Zealand

Penguin Books Ltd, Registered Offices: Harmondsworth, Middlesex, England

First published in the United States of America by Albert Whitman & Company, 1986
Published in Puffin Books 1988
Text copyright © Virginia Mueller, 1986
Illustrations copyright © Lynn Munsinger, 1986
All rights reserved
Library of Congress Cataloging in Publication Data
Mueller, Virginia.
Monster can't sleep/by Virginia Mueller; pictures by Lynn Munsinger.
p. cm.
Summary: Monster can't fall asleep no matter what his parents try
until he tries to put his pet spider to sleep.
ISBN 0-14-050878-3
[1. Bedtime—Fiction. 2. Sleep—Fiction. 3. Monsters—Fiction.] I. Munsinger, Lynn, ill. II. Title.
PZ7.M879Mq 1988 [E]—dc 19 87-32870

Printed in Hong Kong by South China Printing Company

For Ann Fay. *V.M.*
For Doris Dahowski. *L.M.*

Monster was playing with his stuffed spider.

"It's bedtime," said Mother.

But Monster wasn't sleepy.

Father gave Monster some warm milk.

But Monster wasn't sleepy.

Mother read Monster a bedtime story.

But Monster wasn't sleepy.

Mother and Father kissed Monster good night.

But Monster wasn't sleepy.

"It's time for bed," said Mother. "Good night!"

"It's bedtime for Spider, too," said Monster.

He brought Spider some warm milk.

He told Spider a story.

He gave Spider a kiss.

"Good night, Spider," said Monster.

Then Monster went to sleep.